Dreams

Francis Henderson

Illustrations by
Karissa Bettendorf

Handersen Publishing
Lincoln, Nebraska USA

Dreams are stories you see while asleep.

Some dreams are happy or scary or sad
About things forgotten.
About things you had.
About things you wished for
Or times you were bad.

Dreams may be funny and cause you to giggle,

Or see you squirm like a worm with a wiggle.

Or run like a dog with a tail you can wag.

Or snuggle your kitten, too tired to play tag,

Or climb up a fence with sharp barbs that snag.

In dreams you do things that you can't do at all
Like fly over trees, or bounce when you fall
Or look short and pudgy, or skinny and tall,
Or sit still and quiet, or dance up a wall.

Some dreams are happy like birthdays that treat you
Or scary with monsters coming to eat you,
But all disappear from your sleep or your nap
Once you're awakened by a sound or a clap.

Other dreams come not asleep, but awake,

Of great things to do or long trips yet to make.

Or what you will do when you're no longer small
Great things no one ever imagined at all.

Things to help people be healthy or wise.
Or build mighty towers that rise to the skies.

Or write special stories that bring tears to eyes
Or paint magic pictures worthy of prize.

Such dreams as these need not disappear

Keep them within you, treasured and dear.

A seed carefully planted like that will soon seem

To blossom in time as your own special dream.

What are your dreams?

my dreams are _____!

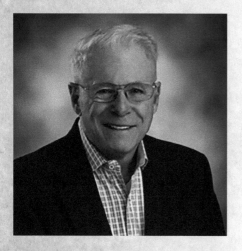

Francis Henderson currently resides in Lincoln, Nebraska after retiring from medical practice claiming to have treated "children of all ages." In 2011, he published "From Presbyterian Hill to Holiday Hill: The Rise and Demise of a Historic Icon." He now writes with an emphasis on children's literature.

Karissa Bettendorf lives in Lincoln, Nebraska, with her husband, little boy, and dog. When she is not painting, she is busy being a mom, gardening, baking, reading, and eating chocolate!

Dreams

Handersen Publishing, LLC
Lincoln, Nebraska USA

Summary: A rhyming story about the dreams children have.

Library of Congress Control Number: 2018908939
Handersen Publishing, LLC, Lincoln, Nebraska

ISBN-13: 978-1-947854-21-5

Handersen Publishing LLC
Great books for young readers
www.handersenpublishing.com

CPSIA information can be obtained
at www.ICGtesting.com
Printed in the USA
BVHW021944060519
547492BV00004B/19/P